DUCKHAMPTON

Written by Christian McLean • Illustrations by Amelia Haviland

DUCKHAMPTON PRESS   FLANDERS, NEW YORK

Published by Duckhampton Press
916 Flanders Road
Flanders, NY 11901

Publisher's Cataloging-in-Publication Data
McLean, Christian.

Duckhampton / written by Christian McLean ; illustrations by Amelia Haviland — Flanders, NY : Duckhampton Press, 2006.

p. ; cm.
Summary: A young duck gets lost on his way from New York City to Duckhampton and makes friends along the way.

ISBN: 0-9771013-0-4
ISBN13: 978-0-9771013-0-6

1. Birds—Fiction. 2. Friendship—Fiction. 3. Prejudices—Fiction. I. Haviland, ill. II. Title.

PZ10.3 .M35Du 2005
[E]—dc22   2005938657

Printed in China
10 09 08 07 06 · 5 4 3 2 1

To Mom and Dad, for giving me the courage to fly

and the love to find my way home.

On a warm spring morning, Mr. and Mrs. Gadwall, of the Gadwalls of Central Park, called their young ducklings in from the Lake. First came Bitsy, then Margaret, followed by Kenneth III, Francis, and finally, trailing behind, was Robert, the smallest of the five. The baby ducks were the spitting image of their parents, with bright white feathers and little turned-up bills.

When the five gathered round, Mr. Gadwall spoke.

"To be a Gadwall," he began, "is to do as Gadwalls do. All birds are different and they must be treated so. The swans are the Kings and Queens of the Park, so you must always show them respect. You can speak to ducks like us, but Gadwalls never talk to pigeons and geese. They are dirty, dangerous, and will steal your feathers."

With that said, the Gadwalls spent the rest of the spring swimming in the cool lake of Central Park and dining at the Boathouse in proper Gadwall fashion.

By late May, it had become too warm in the city and Mr. and Mrs. Gadwall called the ducklings together again.

"Children, it is much, much too hot to stay in Manhattan," Mrs. Gadwall said.

"Tomorrow we will be flying east to Duckhampton for the summer," Mr. Gadwall added.

"What's Duckhampton?" Robert asked.

"Well, I heard from Mrs. Rockefeather that the pond in Duckhampton is the perfect temperature and there are no geese or pigeons. Only swans and ducks like us," said Margaret.

"The Vanderbills say it's better than Boca!" Kenneth added.

"Where's Boca?" Robert asked.

"It's in Florida, honey. It's where we go when it's cold," Mrs. Gadwall said.

That night, the Gadwalls went to bed early so they would have enough energy to fly to Duckhampton in the morning. But Robert stayed up, wondering what Duckhampton would be like. He pictured giant ponds, fresh bread, and hundreds and hundreds of ducks.

Before he knew it, the sun had started to rise and Mr. and Mrs. Gadwall had awakened the rest of the ducklings for the flight to Duckhampton.

Robert followed behind his family as they flew east over Manhattan toward the Brooklyn Bridge, but because he hadn't slept all night, he became tired. No matter how hard he flapped his little wings, he flew slower and slower, until he could no longer keep up with his brothers and sisters.

Suddenly, Robert looked up and his family was gone. Below him, all he could see were pigeons and geese. He was lost in Brooklyn.

Then he saw a sign that read: **TO Queens**. "This must be where the swans live," he thought. "They'll know the way to Duckhampton!"

But when Robert landed, instead of finding swans, he was quickly surrounded by pigeons. He was so afraid, he couldn't move. He couldn't fly. He couldn't run. He just stood still as one of the pigeons approached him.

"What's wrong?" Pigeon asked.

"Please don't steal my feathers," Robert begged.

The pigeons started laughing and Robert became even more frightened.

Pigeon walked closer to Robert.

"What is a Central Park duck like you doing here in Queens?"

"I'm lost. I was on my way to Duckhampton with my family, but I got lost. I'm looking for the swans."

The pigeons started laughing again.

"The swans don't live here. They live up on the North Shore."

"Do you know how to get there? I really need to find them. They'll know the way to Duckhampton," Robert said.

"I can take you to the swans," Pigeon said. "It's not far, but they don't like pigeons very much."

"Please," Robert begged. "I need your help."

Pigeon agreed to help the little duck and after a rest, the two headed north toward the Sound. They flew over Manquackset and then settled by a pond in East Egg.

LONG ISLAND SOUND

ATLANTIC OCEAN

QUEENS

In the pond were a goose and two very old swans. Robert was instantly nervous. He remembered how his parents had warned him about geese, and when Pigeon called Goose over, Robert spread his wings to fly away.

"Where are you going?" Pigeon asked.

"*I'm* not talking to a goose. They're dangerous!"

"They're just birds, like you and me," Pigeon said.

Goose swam up and stuck out his long neck. "Can I help you?" he asked.

"We need to speak with the swans," Pigeon said.

"Those two will never speak to either of you," said Goose. "And all the rest are off in Duckhampton for the summer."

"That's where I'm going!" said Robert. "But I've lost my way. I must speak to the swans. They can help me. I'm sure."

Without another word, Robert swam over to the swans on the opposite shore. "Excuse me, Madam," Robert said.

The two looked at him with his dirty ruffled feathers and kept on their way.

"Excuse me, Sir, I need to get to Duckhampton!" he said.

The swans stopped and studied him for a moment. Then the male swan said, "Old Sport, there is absolutely no way a duck like you could possibly be going to Duckhampton."

"Yes, I am. My name is Robert Gadwall of Central Park and I have lost my family. They said that only swans and ducks like me know the way to Duckhampton."

"I know the Gadwalls of Central Park," the male swan said. "And you, Old Sport, are not one of them. They would not have ruffled feathers or fly with pigeons. No, the Gadwalls of Central Park would not be seen with pigeons at all."

"But I *am* a Gadwall, of the Gadwalls of Central Park. I'm a nephew of Herons and cousin to Larks," Robert said to the old swan.

"I will hear no more of this. If you do not leave us alone, we will be forced to call the police!" the swan said.

When Robert turned and swam back to Pigeon and Goose, a tear appeared in his eye. It ran down his little turned-up bill and dropped into the pond.

"They wouldn't tell me the way," he cried.

"I've been to Duckhampton," Goose said. "I think I can show you the way."

"But you're a *goose*. Geese aren't allowed in Duckhampton," Robert argued.

"I *have* been to Duckhampton. If you want, I will show you where it is, but we must wait until tomorrow. It's getting too late to fly there today."

Meanwhile, in Duckhampton, the Gadwalls had realized that Robert was missing and Mr. Gadwall flew directly to the chief of police. The chief and his deputies searched the skies until dark, but by that time Robert was sound asleep on the shores of East Egg.

Early the next morning, while Robert, Pigeon, and Goose set east toward the rising sun, Mr. Gadwall and the police continued their search for the missing duckling. They flew out to the Lighthouse, then west to East Quack, and still they couldn't find Robert.

That was because Robert was still nowhere near Duckhampton. He was following Goose and Pigeon east, flapping his little wings to keep up.

Suddenly, Robert saw a giant lake, even bigger than the one in Central Park.

"This must be it. Finally, we're here!" he shouted, and flew down to the shore before Goose could stop him.

There were hundreds of ducks of all sizes, shapes, and colors. Robert quickly stopped the first duck he saw and asked for the Gadwalls, but the brown speckled duck looked at him oddly.

"This *is* Duckhampton, is it not?" Robert asked.

"Ronquackama," the duck said. "Duckhampton is east."

Robert grew sad. He wanted to give up, but Goose put his wing around him and said, "I still know the way. It's not far, I promise. We can be there by lunch."

When Robert felt better they were off again, heading due east, looking for ponds or any sign of Duckhampton.

After some time they finally saw what looked like a duck on the side of the road. It was a duck! A giant white duck!

"This must be it! This must be Duckhampton!" Robert shouted. But when they flew closer, there were no ducks. There were no big ponds. No Vanderbills or Rockefeathers.

Then in the distance Robert heard a familiar quack. He looked up and saw Mr. Gadwall, the chief, and his two deputies searching the skies. Robert let out a giant quack and the four ducks flew down to the little duckling.

"Robert, we've found you!" Mr. Gadwall shouted. "We were so worried—but who are these birds with you? A *pigeon* and a *goose*?"

"They're my friends, father."

"No, no, no. Gadwalls are not friends with filthy pigeons and geese. They must have kidnapped you," Mr. Gadwall said.

"No. I got lost and they helped me," Robert argued.

Mr. Gadwall did not believe that a pigeon and a goose could be friends with his son and told the chief to throw the two birds in jail. And so, Robert's two friends were arrested and taken to Duckhampton Jail.

On the beautiful shore of Duckhampton's Great Pond, Robert was finally reunited with his family. They wanted to throw a giant party and invite all the ducks in Duckhampton to celebrate Robert's return, but Robert said, "No."

He did not want a party with all the other ducks in Duckhampton. He just wanted his friends, Pigeon and Goose.

"Please let my friends go," Robert pleaded. "They took care of me when I was alone. They helped when the swans of East Egg laughed at me. I never would have made it here without them. Please let them out—they've done nothing wrong. They may look different, but they're just birds, like you and me."

Mr. Gadwall looked at his son and saw the truth in his words.

"Let them go," Mr. Gadwall shouted to the chief of police, and by the time Robert reached the jail, the two birds had been set free.

That night, grapes were brought from the local vineyards and a party was thrown in proper Duckhampton fashion. But for the first time, it was not in honor of a duck or a swan. It was for a pigeon and a goose.

Dressed in their best, everyone celebrated late into the night, where they ate and sang and even danced together without ruffling a single feather. Because, like Pigeon says, they are all just birds like you and me.

To this day, late in the night, you can still hear the ducks quacking with certain delight. And for those nonbelievers, this story is true, for if you listen quite closely, you might hear honking or even a coo.